The New York Times Best-Selling Series by
Henry Winkler & Lin Oliver

Here's HANK

Everybody Is Somebody

ILLUSTRATED BY SCOTT GARRETT

Penguin Workshop
An Imprint of Penguin Random House

To Indya, Ace, Lulu, Jules, and August.
And always to Stacey—HW

For Henry Winkler, my wonderful
writing partner, who has made this journey
with Hank the trip of a lifetime—LO

For Jakki my sweetheart,
and to Henry and Lin:
Scott Green and I salute you!—SG

PENGUIN WORKSHOP
Penguin Young Readers Group
An Imprint of Penguin Random House LLC

The publisher does not have any control over and does not assume
any responsibility for author or third-party websites or their content.

Text copyright © 2019 by Henry Winkler and Lin Oliver Productions, Inc.
Illustrations copyright © 2019 by Scott Garrett. All rights reserved.
Published by Penguin Workshop, an imprint of Penguin Random House LLC,
345 Hudson Street, New York, New York 10014. PENGUIN and
PENGUIN WORKSHOP are trademarks of Penguin Books Ltd, and
the W colophon is a trademark of Penguin Random House LLC.
Printed in the USA.

Typeset in Dyslexie Font B.V.
Dyslexie Font B.V. was designed by Christian Boer.

Library of Congress Cataloging-in-Publication Data is available.

ISBN 9780515157192 (pbk)   10 9 8 7 6 5 4 3 2
ISBN 9780515157208 (hc)   10 9 8 7 6 5 4 3 2

The books in the Here's Hank series are designed using the font Dyslexie. A Dutch graphic designer and dyslexic, Christian Boer, developed the font specifically for dyslexic readers. It's designed to make letters more distinct from one another and to keep them tied down, so to speak, so that the readers are less likely to flip them in their minds. The letters in the font are also spaced wide apart to make reading them easier.

Dyslexie has characteristics that make it easier for people with dyslexia to distinguish (and not jumble, invert, or flip) individual letters, such as: heavier bottoms (b, d), larger than normal openings (c, e), and longer ascenders and descenders (f, h, p).

This fun-looking font will help all kids—not just those who are dyslexic— read faster, more easily, and with fewer errors. If you want to know more about the Dyslexie font, please visit the site www.dyslexiefont.com.

CHAPTER 1

   "Emily," I said to my sister. "When they take your picture, say 'toenails.'"

   "Eeuw, why would I say 'toenails'?" she answered. "They're gross."

   "Because saying the word moves your lips into a smile," I explained. "Which, I might add, you don't know how to do."

   We were walking down the school hall heading toward the bulletin board where they display the pictures of everyone who wins an award. If you want to be famous, it's the best bulletin board in the school. Every kid at PS 87 has to pass by it at least twice a day.

And today they were taking a picture of Emily to put up on display. She had been picked as Reader of the Month . . . again.

"Hank, you're just jealous because I'm getting my picture up on the bulletin board and you're not," Emily said.

The annoying thing about Emily is that she's always right. I *was* jealous. This was the second time she had been picked as Reader of the Month, this time for having finished thirteen books in thirty days. Ask me how many books I've finished.

The answer is not one.

I want to read, I really do. But my eyes never seem to make friends with the words on the page. All those letters swim around like fish in a pond.

Just once, I'd like to win an award and get my picture pinned right in the center of the board. It could be for anything. Like being the best tuna-fish sandwich eater. I'm really good at that. Or for falling asleep. I can fall asleep before my eyes are even closed.

But no one gives out awards for those things, especially the head of my school, Principal Love. He's got a mole on his cheek that looks just like the Statue of Liberty without the torch. Every time he laughs, it looks like the mole is doing the hula. I bet he wishes they gave out awards for the best mole.

When Emily and I reached the bulletin board, my parents were already there. They had come early to be sure they didn't miss taking even one picture of Emily. They have a whole photo album just for Emily and her awards. Their smiles were so big, you could see every one of their teeth, even the yellow ones in the back.

"Yoo-hoo, kids," my mom shouted. "We're over here!"

My mom always calls out to us

as though we can't see her.
I don't know why she does that.
My eyes are working fine. It's my
brain that doesn't work so well.

Both my parents were wearing the
green buttons our school gives out
that say I'M A PROUD PS 87 PARENT.
I wondered if that meant they were
proud of both of us or just Emily.

"Oh, look," Emily said. "The
whole family is here for my special
day."

"Not exactly," I pointed out. "If you notice, Cheerio's not here."

"Hank, Cheerio is a dog."

"To you. To me, he's my younger furry brother."

"Well, he shouldn't be here. He doesn't appreciate books."

"Are you kidding?" I said. "He loves chewing on them! And the ones he likes the best, he pees on."

Principal Love arrived then, his face lighting up when he saw Emily. The mole on his cheek was dancing up a storm.

"Hello, all you Zipzers!" he said with a big grin. "You're looking very zippy today."

"It's a special day for Emily," my father said.

Principal Love took a key from his pocket and unlocked the glass case protecting the bulletin board. Then he pulled a picture of Emily out of a brown manila envelope.

"Oh, look," he said. "There are already thumbtack holes in the corners of this picture from the last time we put it up."

Emily smiled so big, I thought her face was going to crack in half. All I wanted to do was throw up.

Principal Love tacked Emily's picture onto the center of the bulletin board, right under the big black letters that said

READER OF THE MONTH. He was careful to use the pinholes that were already there. He'd probably get to use them twenty more times before the year was up.

"Time for a photo opportunity," he said as he closed the case. "Your family certainly doesn't want to forget this proud moment."

Maybe the rest of them didn't, but I sure did. My memory is full of proud moments about Emily in school and kind of empty about proud school moments of me.

"Dad, let me take the picture," I said.

I thought that at least taking the picture would give me something to do, rather than just looking like the loser brother standing next to my winner sister.

"Okay, Hank," my dad said, holding out his phone. "You take the picture. And try not to cut off our heads."

I left my mom's side and took the phone. As I snapped the photo, I wondered if the day would ever come when I would get my own special honor.

CHAPTER 2

I didn't think the morning could get worse, but it did. As I was walking to class, Nick the Tick McKelty grabbed my backpack for no reason and tossed it into the trash can. When I reached into the trash to get it out, I grabbed a rotten banana skin, which slimed all over my fingers. I'm not even going to tell you about the old baloney sandwich that was stuck to the banana.

If that wasn't bad enough,

Ms. Flowers surprised us with a pop science quiz on Chapter Four. It's really hard to take a test on Chapter Four when I hadn't even started Chapter Two yet. I'm what you call a slow reader. A snail reads faster than I do.

The worst part of the morning came when Ms. Flowers said we were going to the library. I have nothing against the library. In fact, when I see all those books on the shelves, I wish I could read every one. I imagine stories about wizards, pirates, and people who ride dog sleds across the Arctic and come face-to-face with polar bears. But those stories are made of words, and words are made of

letters that I can't sound out.
All those library books just stay
on the shelf looking down at me.

The one good thing about the
library is Mrs. King, the librarian.
She really tries hard to find books
that I'd like. The last time I was
there, she handed me a book
about penguins in Antarctica. I
tried to read it, but the pictures
in it made me feel so cold, I had
to put on my Mets sweatshirt.

As we walked to the library,
my best friend Ashley was
bubbling over with ideas.

"I can't wait to check out the
next Detective Duck book," she
said. "They're so funny. The last
one quacked me up."

Despite my horrible day, I burst out laughing.

"Finally, there's a smile on your face," my other best friend, Frankie, said. "You've been down in the dumps all morning, Zip."

"How would you feel if your little sister got all the awards and made you feel like you could never do anything right?"

"You do a lot of stuff right," Ashley said. "You're a great friend, and you can tie a cherry stem into a knot with your tongue. I bet Emily can't do that."

By then, we had reached the library. We waited in line while Mrs. King gave us instructions.

"Students," she said. "Feel free to look around and pick a book to check out. Don't just stay in your favorite section. If you like mysteries, try picking a biography. Try something new."

"I'm sticking with Detective Duck," Ashley whispered.

"Remember to use your library voices," Mrs. King went on. "And when you take a book off the shelf, be sure to put it back where it belongs."

We went inside, and all the kids spread out to different sections. Katie Sperling went to the fantasy section in search of unicorns. Ryan Shimozato was looking for sports heroes. Luke Whitman just stood there picking his nose, as usual.

"You don't want to touch a

book that he's touched," Frankie whispered to me. "That finger has been places we never want to go."

"Yeah, and I thought the banana peel in the trash can was slimy," I said.

"I really don't want to know why your hand was in the trash can," Frankie said.

"I can explain," I answered.

"Maybe later," Frankie said. "Or maybe never. Yeah, never works."

Frankie wandered off to the science section. He was looking for a book about robots. I wanted to go to the kindergarten section, because all those books have more pictures than words. I was too embarrassed, so instead I pulled out a book about George Washington. I opened it up and stared at a picture of him in his white wig and fancy clothes.

"Hank, I didn't know you were interested in history," a voice behind me said. It was Mr. Rock, our music teacher and all-around cool guy.

"I can't put this book down," I said to him.

"Really? Is it that good?"

"No, but the person who read it before me must have had a peanut-butter sandwich, because the cover is stuck to my hands."

Mr. Rock cracked up, which surprised me. I didn't even know I was being funny.

"Hank, you have a great sense of humor," Mr. Rock said. "Come with me, and I'll show you some books I think you'd really like."

I pulled the book off my hands, wiped the peanut butter onto my jeans, and followed him to a display table. He picked up a book and showed me the cover, which had two kids dressed in white space suits.

"This book is full of adventure, but it's funny, too," Mr. Rock said. "It's written by a wonderful author, Paula Hart. She's a friend of mine, and I asked her to come speak at our school on Friday."

"I've never met a real author," I said.

"You're going to love this book," Mr. Rock said. "Even the title is great, don't you think?"

I looked at the title.

"*Journey to Japan*," I read aloud. "I bet this book has a lot of pictures of volcanoes. I saw a TV show that said there are over two hundred volcanoes in Japan."

"Hank," Mr. Rock said. "The cover says *Journey to Jupiter*, not

Journey to Japan. It's about a bunch of kids who set up the first space colony on the planet Jupiter."

"Oh, Jupiter, of course," I said. "That makes sense. That's why the kids are both dressed in white space suits."

Mr. Rock rubbed his chin like he was thinking. Then he said, "Hank, do you have trouble reading?"

I laughed, a little too hard.

"You can tell me if reading is difficult for you," he went on. "You're not alone, you know."

"Well, sometimes I just get the *j* words mixed up," I said, not telling the whole truth. "You know, like Jupiter, Japan, giraffe."

"Giraffe starts with a *g*, not a *j*," Mr. Rock said.

I definitely did not want to continue this conversation. I wanted to get out of there as fast as I could.

"I'm going to go check this book out right now," I said to Mr. Rock. "I'll let you know how I like it."

"I have another idea," Mr. Rock said. "Ms. Adolf, Principal Love, and I are going to select some students to welcome Paula Hart to our school. The winners will introduce her at the assembly, show her around **PS** 87, and make her feel at home. Why don't you try out? I think you'd do a great job."

"That sounds incredible," I said. "Maybe my friends Ashley and Frankie can try out, too?"

"Why not? You'd be a welcoming trio."

This was exciting. "What do we have to do?" I asked.

"The rules have been posted on the bulletin board outside Principal Love's office for two weeks now," he said. "I take it you didn't read them."

"I usually walk really fast when I'm near Principal Love's

office," I said. "Just in case he wants to call me in and discuss my grades."

Mr. Rock laughed.

"That makes sense to me," he said. "So all you have to do is read the book and come to the tryouts tomorrow. Then tell us what you liked about the book in your own words."

"Does that mean I have to read the whole book?" I asked. "Like, start at the first page and go all the way to the end?"

Mr. Rock laughed again. "That's usually the way a book is read. Trust me, Hank. Once you start, you won't be able to put down this book."

Mr. Rock sure didn't know the inside of my brain.

I had at least a million reasons why I couldn't read that book. In fact, there were so many that I couldn't possibly list them all here. So I'm only going to give you four.

CHAPTER 3

FOUR REASONS WHY I COULDN'T READ *JOURNEY TO JUPITER*

(OR ANY BOOK, FOR THAT MATTER)

BY HANK ZIPZER

1. When I look at a page in a book, all I see are letters swimming around like big red Swedish Fish. And what good are Swedish Fish if you can't eat them?

2. My eyes are allergic to reading. They don't sneeze. They just refuse to stay open.

3. When I try to read, my mind immediately goes on vacation. Once it went scuba diving for buried treasure right in the middle of a chapter on megamouth sharks.

4. I don't even know what reason Number 4 is. I just know that reading makes me itchy all over.

CHAPTER 4

It was Fish Stick Delight Day in the cafeteria, which meant that the entire lunchroom smelled like the bottom of a fishing boat. Frankie, Ashley, and I waited in line, pushing our trays forward with one hand and holding our noses with the other. I had put *Journey to Jupiter* on my lunch tray, thinking that maybe if I kept it close, the words would magically fly into my brain.

"Let me get this straight, Zip,"

Frankie said, as he took a plate of fish sticks and peas and put them on his tray. "Mr. Rock asked you to try out to be on the welcoming committee for Paula Hart, but you've decided not to? That doesn't make any sense."

"No," I answered. "What doesn't make sense is the fact that I'd have to read her whole book by tomorrow. There's no way I could do that."

I grabbed my plate of fish sticks, but the book took up so much room on my tray, there was barely a place to put it down. It didn't matter, anyway, because a large sweaty hand came swooping in and snatched the plate right

out of my hands. The large sweaty
hand belonged to the large sweaty
Nick McKelty.

"You snooze, you lose,
Zipperbutt," he said as he stuffed
one of the fish sticks into his
mouth. "Your lunch belongs to me."

"Give Hank his lunch back,"
Ashley said. "That is disgusting,
taking food off other people's
trays."

McKelty didn't answer. He just opened his mouth and let out one of his snorty rhino laughs. We could see the fish flakes squeezing through the gap between his front teeth. It was enough to make me lose my appetite.

"That's okay, Ashley," I said. "I'm not hungry anymore."

I filled my tray with three cups of diced peaches and headed for our usual table. Frankie and Ashley followed. We sat down, being careful not to sit too close to McKelty. He was at the table next to us, sucking in a giant pile of food like a vacuum cleaner.

"Back to Paula Hart," Frankie

said. "She writes the coolest books. I've read them all."

"Me too," Ashley said. "They're not that hard, Hank. Try it. Open the book and read the first couple of sentences."

I took the book off my tray and opened it to Chapter One. I stared at the first sentence for a long time. Here is what was written:

Dressed in their white space suits, Sarah and James looked out the portal of their rocket and gazed down at Jupiter.

I cleared my throat and read aloud.

"Dressing in whale steamships, Susan and James grazed out the pothole at Jupiter."

Frankie and Ashley looked at each other without a word.

"How'd I do?" I asked. Judging from the looks on their faces, I wasn't too hopeful.

"Well, it was definitely interesting," Frankie said.

"And very creative," Ashley added.

"But I wasn't trying to be

creative," I explained. "I was just trying to read the words on the page. And I didn't, right?"

Ashley and Frankie shook their heads.

"See," I said. "I told you I can't read."

I heard a loud rhino snort from the table next to us.

"That's because you're stupid, Zipperteeth," McKelty yelled. "You can't do anything right."

Ashley and Frankie jumped up and marched right over to Mrs. Crock, who was on lunchroom duty.

"Nick McKelty is calling Hank names," Frankie said. And before you could say Fish Stick Delight,

Mrs. Crock was escorting Nick McKelty out of the cafeteria. There is no name calling allowed at PS 87.

"Don't pay any attention to McKelty," Ashley said after he was gone. "You can do anything you want to do, Hank."

"Except be on the welcoming committee for Paula Hart."

"That's not the worst thing in the world," Frankie said. "The only thing you'll miss is not getting your picture on the big bulletin board."

I nearly choked on my diced peaches.

"What did you say?" I asked Frankie.

"I said that the welcoming committee gets their picture on the big bulletin board by the entrance. It says so on the poster for tryouts."

The poster! There's another thing I can't read.

"Oh man, I want my picture up there more than anything," I said. "Just once, I'd like to show Emily that I can get a special honor, too."

"Hey, we're here to help," Ashley said. "What's the plan?"

"Well, Mr. Rock said we could be a trio. How about if you guys try out with me and help me do what I can't do?"

"There's not much time. The

tryouts are tomorrow," Frankie said.

"What are you doing after school today?" I asked.

"I was going to make dumplings with my grandma," Ashley said.

"And I was going to play catch with my brother," Frankie said.

"Well, say goodbye to dumplings and baseball," I said. "Let's meet in the basement clubhouse. Are you in?"

"In!" Frankie said. "I'll tell my brother that we'll play catch tomorrow instead."

"And I'll tell Grandma something really important came

up," Ashley said. "She always understands."

"Great. Then the first meeting of the Get-Our-Pictures-on-the-Bulletin-Board Club will start at four o'clock sharp."

I had no idea what we were going to do at that meeting.

All I knew was that I would bring my mom's chocolate-chip cookies and a jar of Papa Pete's pickles, and that was a good start.

CHAPTER 5

At exactly four o'clock that afternoon, we met in the basement of our apartment building. Our clubhouse is really a storeroom next to the laundry room. People keep furniture and boxes there that they don't want in their apartments. There's also a comfortable old flowered couch we love to sit on. The only thing is, if you flop down on it too hard, you could disappear in all the dust that flies out of its cushions.

I put a tin of chocolate-chip cookies and a jar of pickles down on the cardboard box we use for a table.

"No one eats cookies and pickles together," Frankie said, making a face.

"You don't eat them together," I explained. "First, you take a mouthful of cookie. You swallow it, then go in for the pickle. Sweet, sour, sweet, sour. Trust me, your tongue is going to stand up and dance."

Frankie and Ashley tried my cookie-pickle combo, but it wasn't a big hit.

"Ewww," they both said at once.

"Okay then, let's get down to business," I said. "Mr. Rock said that for the tryouts, we have to say what we liked about *Journey to Jupiter*. I actually have a couple of things I did like."

"That's a good start," Frankie said. "Like what?"

"Yes, tell us, Mr. Zipzer," Ashley said, imitating a teacher's voice.

I stood up and held the book in my hands like I was giving an oral report.

"First of all, I like the color of the cover," I began. "I think books with purple covers have the best stories. And I like the smell of the paper. I also like that there are illustrations. Most of all, I like that when you put this book down on top of a bunch of papers, it stops them from blowing away in the wind."

"But, Hank," Ashley said in a supportive voice. "You have to tell what the story is about."

"That's a problem, because I haven't read the book," I said, flopping down onto the couch. That created a dust storm right there in the storage room. We all sneezed at once.

"We can help you with that, Zip," Frankie said. "Just start reading it aloud, and we'll help you with the words you don't know."

"Good idea," I said. "We'll be done with the book about two years from next Christmas."

"That's a good point," Ashley said. "We are up against a time crunch here. So maybe we should just tell you all about the book."

"Yeah," Frankie said. "Knowing the story will make it much easier for you to read it on your own." Ashley began.

"The book starts when Sarah and James arrive at the first space colony on Jupiter," she said. "Before they can settle in, they come face-to-face with a horrible creature they've never seen before."

"It's huge and angry," Frankie went on, "and chases them into the center of a superstorm. All of a sudden, it grabs them and holds them close to its sticky chest."

"Wow, that sounds so scary," I said.

"Yeah," Ashley agreed. "But the funny part is that the creature is sucking on a baby bottle filled with purple slime. And when the creature burps, it splatters the slime all over Sarah's helmet."

"Which means that she can't see the glowing space pirate riding toward her on a giant spoon," Frankie added.

The story was interrupted by a loud knock on the door. I nearly jumped out of my skin.

"There's a space pirate at the door," I said, with a shiver.

It wasn't a space pirate.

It was Ashley's grandma, and by the way, she wasn't riding a spoon.

"Ashley, I've been looking all over for you," she said. "The dumplings are ready to be stuffed." Then she turned to Frankie. "And your mother said for me to tell you your brother is waiting to play ball."

"Looks like we have to go," Ashley said.

"But what about the rest of the story?" I asked.

"Zip, we're so sorry," Frankie said. "Ask someone in your family to help you read the rest of the book. Ask your dad."

Right. There's a good idea. His other name is Mr. Patience.

We all rode up in the elevator together. Ashley and her grandma got off at the third floor. Frankie got off at the fourth, and I rode all the way to the tenth floor by myself.

"Hey, Dad," I said as I walked into the apartment. "Can you help me with something?"

He was sitting at the dining-room table in front of his computer. That's where he works.

"I just have a minute," he said, never taking his eyes off his computer screen. "I've got to get this report in today."

I knew reading *Journey to Jupiter* would take more than a minute. In fact, it might take more than a year.

"That's okay, Dad. I'll figure it out on my own."

I slipped into my room. Cheerio followed me.

"Okay, Cheerio, it's you and me," I said, taking *Journey to Jupiter* out of my backpack. "This is called a book. I know you want to chew it, but you can't because I have to read it."

Cheerio sat down on the rug, and I sat down in my desk chair.

"This book takes place on Jupiter," I began.

Cheerio yawned.

"I'm going to ask you not to yawn again," I told him. "It's not good for my confidence."

I pointed to the picture on the cover.

"This is Sarah. And this is James."

Cheerio yawned again, this time letting out a little yip.

"Cheerio, didn't I just ask you not to do that? Come on, give a guy a break. Now, pay attention because I'm going to read the first page. And after that, I only have one hundred twenty-seven more to read."

I cleared my throat and began. "*Journey to Jupiter* by Paula Hart, with illustrations by Scott Green."

That's as far as I got. All of a sudden, Cheerio keeled over onto the rug. I mean, he went from being wide awake to snoring like a bear.

"Okay, Hank," I said to myself. "You can read this book on your own. Other people do."

I moved from my chair to my bed, fluffed up my pillow, and put it behind my back. I took the book in my hands and turned to Chapter One.

That's the last thing I remember, because in no time, I was snoring like a bear, too.

CHAPTER 6

If you're wondering if I finished *Journey to Jupiter*, you can stop wondering now. The answer is a big fat no. It's not that I didn't want to read it. I saw the letters on the page; I just couldn't sound them out.

That's why when Frankie, Ashley, and I walked into the tryouts the next day, I wasn't feeling my most confident. We took our seats on the big colorful carpet in the middle of the library, the place where Mrs. King holds all our reading assemblies.

We whispered to one another, making a plan that we hoped would work.

"I'll start," Ashley whispered, "because I can summarize the story really well."

"I'll go next," Frankie said. "I'll tell all about the main characters. Zip, you can wrap it up."

"What am I going to say?" I whispered in a panic. "You know I haven't finished the book yet."

"Where are you up to?" Ashley asked.

"The middle of page one," I answered.

The library door opened, and the judges walked in. There was Ms. Adolf, who, as always, was dressed all in gray. Her skirt was gray, her shoes were gray, her hair was gray, even her knees were gray. Principal Love followed her, his Velcro sneakers squeaking all the way across the library floor. Last was Mr. Rock, who smiled and waved at all the kids as he bounced in.

They sat down and called up the first person. She was Grace I-don't-remember-her-last-name, a third-grader who used so many big words she sounded like a walking dictionary. Ms. Adolf was so impressed that I thought I saw a smile trying to escape from her lips.

The next people to try out were two girls from the third grade. They giggled from the moment they stood up until Principal Love asked them to step into the hall to get control of themselves. They never came back.

After them was Luke Whitman, who is actually a very good reader. It's one of the few things he can do with one hand while picking his nose with the other. After Luke was Heather Payne, the tallest girl in our class, who does everything perfectly. Of course, she did a perfect job.

"How are we going to follow that?" I whispered to Frankie and Ashley, sinking lower in my seat.

"Do you want to get your picture on that bulletin board or not?" Frankie asked.

That's all I needed to hear. I got fired up and ready to go, which was a good thing, because we were next.

When we stood in front of the judges, I flashed my best smile, the one filled with my Zipzer attitude. Ms. Adolf stared at me like she had just licked a sour lemon. Ashley and Frankie each did an amazing job of describing the plot and the main characters. Then it was my turn.

"You don't need to hear me discuss *Journey to Jupiter*," I began, "because my teammates already covered that. Instead, I'm going to discuss how we can show Paula Hart the best time ever, here at PS 87."

Mr. Rock gave me an encouraging smile.

"First of all, we could give her some pickles from my mom's deli, because everyone loves a dill pickle. We could be very polite and thank her for visiting us. We could make her laugh. For instance, I have a great joke about Jupiter. Want to hear it?"

"No," said Ms. Adolf.

"Yes," said Mr. Rock.

I didn't wait
for Principal Love
to answer.

"Knock, knock," I said.

"Who's there?" said Mr. Rock.

"Jupiter," I said with a grin.

"Jupiter who?"

"Ju-pi-ter hurry, or you'll miss
the bus."

Mr. Rock cracked up. I could
tell Principal Love liked it because
the mole on his cheek did the
hula. The other kids in the library
laughed out loud. Only Ms. Adolf
didn't crack a smile.

"There is no laughing in the
library," she growled. "In fact,
this team is out of the running
for being too silly."

"Not so fast, Ms. Adolf," Mr. Rock said. "I know Paula Hart, and she's a very funny person. She puts humor in all her books. I think she'd get a big kick out of Hank and his team. They're my first choice."

Wow. I couldn't believe my ears. My eyes moved to Principal Love. He was going to be the deciding vote. I wish I understood what he said next.

"Humor is also known by the word 'comedy,'" he began. "It is the opposite of drama, which is serious and does not involve laughter. Yet it seems to me that the visit of Paula Hart is an appropriate occasion for laughter, which also helps with the digestion of vegetables."

"Is he saying yes or no?" I whispered to Frankie and Ashley.

"Whatever he's saying, he's taking a long time," Ashley whispered back.

"While I usually agree with Ms. Adolf," Principal Love went on, "in this case, I have to go with Mr. Rock."

It was a yes.

Three of my favorite letters.

Y. E. S.

I could already see that bulletin board in my mind. There was my picture, grinning at everyone who passed by.

Get ready, bulletin board. Here I come!

CHAPTER 7

On Friday, Frankie, Ashley, and I got all dressed up in our best clothes, the ones that our parents make us wear when we go out to dinner with them. It was very uncomfortable sitting in class wearing my blue suit. It made me feel like I wanted to scratch all over.

Finally, at eleven o'clock, Ms. Flowers dismissed us so that we could go welcome Paula Hart. We hurried down the hall to the entrance of our school.

Principal Love stood on the steps with us as we waited for Paula Hart to arrive. I was excited to meet a real author. I was nervous, too, knowing that I hadn't finished her book yet. In fact, I still hadn't finished Chapter One.

A yellow taxi pulled up in front of our school. Before the door opened, a woman with purple streaks in her hair poked her head out of the window.

"Hi, kids!" she shouted. "Is this PS 87?"

"Yes, it is," we shouted back.

"Well, then I'm in the right place," she said with a big laugh.

The taxi door flew open, and

out came Paula Hart. The first thing I noticed was her shoes—pink, glittery army boots with purple shoelaces. She had silver rings on every finger and a long dress with giraffes all over it. You couldn't miss her earrings, which were sparkly books covered with red rhinestones.

"Oh my gosh," Ms. Hart said, walking right up to Ashley. "I love your rhinestone glasses. As far as I'm concerned, a person can't sparkle enough."

Ashley giggled so much, she forgot what she was supposed to say. Frankie stuck his hand out and jumped into the conversation.

"Welcome to our school," he said to Ms. Hart. "I'm Frankie Townsend, and this is Ashley Wong and Hank Zipzer. We're the welcoming committee. We are all looking forward to hearing you speak."

"My oh my, you have a great handshake," Ms. Hart said,

pumping Frankie's arm so hard
it made his head jiggle.

"Hey, look," I said to her.
"You turned my best friend into
a bobblehead doll. Maybe I can
put him on the shelf with my
baseball-player collection. I have
six bobbleheads. I got the last
one when my grandpa took me
to a Mets night game."

I felt Principal Love's hand
land like a jet plane on my
shoulder.

"Hank," he said. "I'm sure
Ms. Hart does not want to hear
the details of your toy collection."

"Are you kidding me?"
Ms. Hart said. "I am a huge fan
of bobblehead dolls. I have a really

cool hula dancer standing right next to my computer and a jiggly wiener dog on my kitchen windowsill."

"I have a wiener dog, too," I said. "But he's real. And his name is Cheerio. I named him that because when he chases his tail, he spins in a circle and looks like a Cheerio."

Ms. Hart laughed so hard that I thought the sixth-grade class on the third floor could hear her.

"I like you, Hank," she said. "You're funny. I was a funny kid, too, which always got me into trouble with my teachers."

"Me too," I whispered. She gave me a fist bump.

"From now on, call me Paula," she said. And then she winked at me.

"The second- and third-grade classes are waiting for us in the library," Principal Love said. "Children, let's show Ms. Hart the way."

He turned and led us into school and down the main hall to the library. We passed the bulletin board with my sister's face plastered right in the middle of it. The hall was quiet, and we could hear Principal Love's Velcro sneakers squeaking across the floor.

"It sounds like he's got a live mouse in his shoes," Paula whispered to us.

We covered our mouths so we didn't laugh too loud. Principal Love glanced over his shoulder with a look that said, "Behave yourselves." That look even wiped the smile off Paula Hart's face. When we reached the library, the Queen of Wipe-That-Smile-Off-Your-Face, Ms. Adolf, was waiting in the doorway.

"I'm glad you're finally here," Ms. Adolf said. "I've had a hard time keeping the children sitting still on the rug."

"That's okay," Paula said.

"They can squirm a little. I don't mind."

"I'm kind of squirmy myself," I piped up.

"It's not something to brag about, Henry," Ms. Adolf said.

Mr. Rock came right over to Paula and gave her a hug and a smile. They looked like they were good friends, and I could see why. They were both really cool people.

We went inside the library. Mrs. King was standing at the front, with a huge smile on her face. She's a person who loves books, and anything that has to do with them. Paula waved and all the second- and third-graders cheered. I took a bow and everyone laughed, including Paula, Mrs. King, and Mr. Rock.

"Who's introducing me?" Paula asked.

"I will," I answered. I spun around and checked with Frankie and Ashley. "If it's okay with you guys, that is."

"Go ahead, Hank," Ashley said. "You'll do a great job."

Paula flashed me a big smile.

"Take it away, Hank," she said.

I stood on my tiptoes in front of the microphone.

"Today we are lucky to have a famous author with us. She writes great books for kids, and I just found out that she's also really funny. Let's give a warm PS 87 welcome to Paula Hart."

Everyone clapped. Frankie, Ashley, and I sat down in the front row. Paula started her speech, which wasn't really a speech. She talked to us like we were just hanging around having a pizza together. She didn't even use notes. She read us an exciting chapter from *Journey to Jupiter*.

Afterward, Frankie and Ashley asked for questions. Heather Payne put up her hand.

"What made you want to become a writer?" she asked.

"I always knew deep down that I wanted to be a writer," Paula said. "I loved to daydream about exciting adventures. Other kids thought I was weird. But a very smart teacher told me to pay attention to the voice inside that made me special, no matter what other people thought."

Everyone listened carefully except **Nick McKelty**. He just let out another one of his rhino snorts and shouted, "**Zipzer** should know all about that. He's weird."

My face turned red, and I wanted to disappear. Thank goodness for Paula Hart.

"Maybe Hank will be a writer when he grows up," she said, smiling at me. "He's certainly original enough."

My face turned red again, but this time, I was blushing because I was proud.

"Before we take more questions," Paula said, "I want

you to hear something very important. You all have greatness in you. You don't know what you can accomplish until you try. Now, who's got another question?"

Of course, Nick McKelty's hand shot up.

"My question is for Hank Zipzer," he said.

"He's a very interesting person," said Paula. "I have a lot of questions for him myself. Hank, come on up here and share the stage with me."

I took my place next to her. I didn't have a good feeling about this.

"My favorite part of *Journey to Jupiter* was Chapter Five," McKelty began. "I want to know what Zipzer thought about that chapter, when James surprised Sarah with his plan."

I realized what McKelty was up to. He knew I have trouble reading and hadn't finished the book. He was just trying to trick me and embarrass me again. But I wasn't going to let him get away with that.

"Actually, Nick, I have to disagree with you," I said. "I think Chapter Six was much more exciting. Especially the way it ended."

Take that, Nick McKelty,

I thought to myself. I was happy to see him shut his slobbery mouth and put his beefy hand down. But I wasn't prepared for what happened next.

Paula Hart broke into a big smile.

"That's amazing, Hank," she said. "Because Chapter Six is my favorite, too. Tell me, what part did you think was most exciting?"

Oh no!

I could feel every eyeball in the library looking at me, waiting for me to answer. The kids. Ms. Adolf. Mr. Rock. Principal Love. Frankie and Ashley. And most of all, Paula Hart.

My heart felt like it was falling out of my chest and down to my feet.

I took a deep breath. I opened my mouth. And the only thing that came out was a gulp.

CHAPTER 8

It felt like I stood there for at least two weeks, with a big spotlight shining right on me. In the background, I could hear Ms. Adolf saying, "Henry, we're waiting, and we don't have all day. Answer the question."

I looked over at Frankie and Ashley in the front row, hoping they could send me brain waves filled with details of Chapter Six. But there was nothing they could do. My whole body had turned ice cold, which is what happens to me when I'm really scared.

Think, Hank. Think of something. Anything.

I figured I had several choices. I could bolt out of the room and run all the way to Peru and ride llamas for the rest of my life. I could admit in front of everyone that I hadn't even finished the first chapter of *Journey to Jupiter.*

Ouch.

Or I could go for it.

And since I'm a go-for-it kind of guy, I went for it. I knew nothing about Chapter Six, or Seven, or Eight for that matter, but I wasn't going to let that stop me.

"What I love about Chapter Six,"

I began, "is that it is in between Chapter Five and Chapter Seven."

Everyone in the audience laughed, especially Paula Hart.

"Oh, Hank," she said. "Everything you say is so original."

That gave me the confidence to go on. I could feel my body warming up and my tongue starting to move.

"I thought the most exciting part was when James and Sarah entered the Cave of Doom and saw that the ground looked alive," I began. "And it was because thousands of space insects covered every inch of the cave floor. They had poisonous stingers, and if one of them bit you, you would grow hair out of your eyes."

I looked over at Paula, and she didn't say a word, so I went on.

"When a whole colony of the space insects crawled up James's leg, Sarah went into battle, swatting them off with her thick glove. They tried to eat their way into her space suit until she attacked them with the laser beam that shot out of the top of her helmet."

Paula got a big smile on her face, and I thought I was home free. My imagination had personality, and it had saved me again.

Then I heard McKelty's voice.

"What book did you read?" he hollered. "There aren't any space insects in *Journey to Jupiter*."

"No, there aren't," answered

Paula, "but there sure should have been. What Hank just described was much more exciting than my Chapter Six."

"It was?" I said. My ears couldn't believe what they were hearing. "Should I go on?"

Before I knew it, Ms. Adolf was standing next to me, wedged in between Paula and me. She was so close, I could smell her grayness.

"On behalf of PS 87," she said, "I would like to apologize for Mr. Zipzer's disrespectful behavior. Clearly, he made up this silly story. He has no business filling the room with such nonsense."

"With all respect, Ms. Adolf, I have to disagree with you," Paula said. "True, Hank didn't tell the story I wrote, but he told his own story. I admire his creativity. Creativity is a gift, don't you think, Mr. Rock?"

"It certainly is," Mr. Rock answered. "As a music teacher, it's what I look for most in my students. You can't make any kind of art without letting your imagination loose."

Ms. Adolf's gray face turned beet red, like she was a balloon about to pop.

"All this talk about creativity and imagination," she grumbled. "This is school, not playtime."

Then she turned and stared at me like she could see right through me.

"Young man, you did not do what you were asked to do," she said. "You did not take your assignment seriously. Imagination is not always enough."

"Actually," Paula said, "imagination is everything when you are a writer. I see a future writer in Hank. That boy tells an exciting story, don't you think, kids?"

Everyone nodded.

"I really liked those space bugs," said Luke Whitman from the back of the room.

"And I liked that Sarah saved James," Heather Payne said. "It's cool when a girl gets to save a boy."

"I can't wait to hear what happens next," Ryan Shimozato said.

"Yeah, Hank, tell us more," Katie Sperling shouted out.

"Hank, do you know what happens next?" Paula asked me.

"No, but I can make it up," I answered.

"That's what writers do," she said. "The world is waiting

to hear your stories, Hank Zipzer.
Never forget that."

All the kids in the library
started to clap. Frankie and Ashley
led a cheer that said, "Go, Hank
Zipzer! Go, Hank Zipzer!" Mr. Rock
gave me a thumbs-up. The only
two sour faces in the room were
Ms. Adolf's and Nick McKelty's.

But I didn't care even a little bit.
Suddenly, my head was swimming
with stories. I felt like a writer,
and trust me, that felt very cool.

CHAPTER 9

A MILLION STORIES THAT POPPED RIGHT INTO MY HEAD

BY HANK ZIPZER

1. The Pickle That Ran for President . . . and Kept on Running

2. How the Raisin Lost Its Wrinkles

3. Oscar: the Amazing Octopus Who Juggled Couch Pillows

I'd tell you even more stories, but my brain doesn't have any more room because it's thinking that it needs a tuna sandwich . . . no tomatoes, of course.

CHAPTER 10

After the assembly, all the kids gathered around me, asking about what happens next in my story.

"Where do all the space bugs go?" Katie asked.

"Do Sarah and James blast them into outer space with their laser beams?" Ryan asked.

"I bet their blood is green and slimy, like snot," Luke Whitman said.

I have to admit, it was fun to be in the spotlight. I hadn't

gotten so much attention since
I threw up cake frosting at my
four-year-old birthday party. Boy,
that was messy. One minute, no
one was looking at me. The next,
everybody was running at me with
paper towels.

I lowered my voice and told all
the kids to lean in close. I didn't
expect them to get that close.

"Hey, guys, give the man some
breathing room," Frankie said.

"Yes," Ashley added. "Hank's
creativity needs space."

"Okay," I began, "here's what
happens next. The space bugs start
to vibrate and make a high sound
like a screeching siren. Then a rock
turtle, found only on Jupiter, falls

from the ceiling of the cave. This kind of turtle has no shell, just dry, cracked skin."

"Eeuuw," said Katie Sperling. "That's gross."

"You haven't heard anything yet," I said. "The space bugs sting the turtle, and hair sprouts from its skin and eyeballs. It looks like it has a shell of hair."

"A hair shell," said Luke Whitman. "That's cool."

From the corner of my eye, I could see Ms. Adolf stomping over to us. I knew I had to wrap up the story fast.

"So then, the space bugs swarm underneath the turtle and lift it off the ground. They carry it deep into the darkness of the cave, and it was never seen again."

Unfortunately, Ms. Adolf heard that last part of my story. Let's just say she wasn't a fan of hairy turtles.

"Henry," she said sternly. "Principal Love is waiting for you in front of the WELCOME, PAULA HART sign. Now follow me, and stop wasting time."

"Come on, Zip," Frankie said. "This is when we get our picture with Paula Hart."

He didn't have to say that twice. I was super ready.

"I've got to go," I said to all the kids. "I'll tell you more later."

Frankie, Ashley, and I hurried down the hall after Ms. Adolf. Principal Love was standing in front of the colorful welcome sign, chatting with Paula and holding his camera.

"Hey, kids," Paula said. "Was that assembly fun, or what?"

"The most fun ever," I answered, and I meant it.

"Let's get on with the picture," Principal Love said. "Ms. Hart has a plane to catch. She's visiting another school in Seattle."

"Lucky kids," Ashley said.

"Ms. Hart, you stand in the middle, and kids, you gather around her," Principal Love suggested. As I took my place next to Paula, I started to smell something bad, like someone had burped up a rotten banana. It didn't seem like a burp that

Paula Hart would make. It was more like a Nick the Tick burp.

Oh no!

I turned around and there he was, in all his stinky rotten banana-ness.

"I thought I'd come and add some good looks to this picture," McKelty said. As the words came out of his mouth, so did his hot breath all over my neck.

"You're not invited, Nick," Frankie said.

"Please step to the side, Nicholas," Ms. Adolf snapped.

"Fine with me," McKelty answered. "I don't want to be

in a picture with Zipperbutt, anyway. His face is going to break the camera."

That did it for me. I had been feeling so good from the assembly, and I wasn't about to let this turkey ruin my moment, my day, or my year.

"You know what I think, McKelty?" I said. "I think you're mean right down to your toes. You must know what it feels like to be called names. I don't understand why you call me names every single day. All I know is it stops here and now."

"Way to stand up for yourself," Paula Hart whispered, giving me a fist bump.

"I'm going to call you anything I want," McKelty said, putting his nose in my face. "And there's nothing you can do about it."

"Here's what I can do about it," Principal Love said. "I'm going to put you in detention for a week with Ms. Adolf. She'll teach you how to control your mouth. Won't you, Ms. Adolf?"

"Oh, you can count on it," she snarled. "Come with me, Nicholas. I have many wastebaskets for you to empty. And that's just the beginning."

As Ms. Adolf guided McKelty back to her classroom, Nick the Tick shot me a look that said, "I'm tough." But I shot a look right back that said, "I'm tougher."

We took about ten pictures with Paula. The first few were regular. Then Paula suggested that we all make a scared face. Then a surprised face. Then a funny face. Then a goofy face. Then it was time for her to go.

Just before she left, she hugged each of us. When it was time for my hug, she whispered in my ear.

"I believe in you, Hank," she said.

Then she swooped off, her giraffe dress and pink boots disappearing down the hall.

I knew I would never forget her.

CHAPTER 11

The whole next week seemed like it took forever to happen. I had actual dreams about standing in front of the bulletin board, watching my picture get put up. In my dreams, I was six feet tall and sitting on a white horse. The horse and I both took a bow as the entire school cheered my name. One of the best parts of the dream was when Ms. Adolf presented me with a bouquet of flowers.

On the actual day, I'm sorry to say there was no white horse involved, and no flowers, either. But I did wear the brand-new red sneakers that my grandpa, Papa Pete, bought me just for my special day.

Principal Love arranged for us all to meet after school. Ashley came with her mom and dad, Dr. and Dr. Wong. Frankie came with his mother and father and his big brother, Otis. They were all wearing T-shirts that said GO, FRANKIE. My mom and dad were wearing the green buttons that say I'M A PROUD PS 87 PARENT. Usually they wear those for Emily's events, but this time, the buttons were for me. That was pretty cool.

Our group included the whole Zipzer family: Mom, Dad, Papa Pete, and Emily, who came with her iguana, Katherine. As always, Katherine was wrapped around Emily's neck like a short green scarf.

"Who invited the lizard?" I asked when I spotted Katherine.

"Katherine's feelings would be hurt if I left her home," Emily said. "Katherine is very sensitive."

"How do you think Cheerio feels," I asked, "being in the apartment all by himself? Poor guy. I wish he was here."

Papa Pete cleared his throat a couple of times to get my attention.

"Look at this, Hankie," he whispered. He slowly unzipped his red sweatshirt just enough for me to see a cute little wet nose poking out from his chest.

"You brought Cheerio?" I whispered.

"He wouldn't miss this for
anything," Papa Pete said.
"Don't tell. It's our secret."

Then he winked at me, and
I winked back, except I'm not
good at winking so both eyes
closed instead of just one.

We heard Principal Love
coming down the hall before
we saw him. His sneakers were
especially loud as they squeaked

toward us. I wondered if his sneakers have a special button that lets him turn up the squeak.

"Well, hello, everyone," he said, taking a brown manila envelope from his jacket. "We're here to celebrate a special moment for these three young people. And as I always say, childhood is a time to climb the mountain of moments until you reach the moment of adulthood. And what a moment that is."

I wish he would get to the moment of putting up our picture!

I looked around at all our

families. They seemed just as confused as we were. They weren't used to hearing Principal Love's speeches, which are even longer than a spider monkey's tail. And he still wasn't finished.

"You children have represented PS 87 in the best possible light," he went on. "You showed Paula Hart what a warm welcome is all about. Ashley and Frankie, you were your usual outstanding selves. And Hank, you certainly added your own personal touch to the event."

I was standing there, thinking that I couldn't listen to one more word. But when I realized he was talking about me, suddenly his speech wasn't so bad. In fact, I was really liking it.

Then came the best part.

Principal Love opened the brown envelope and took out the picture. It showed Frankie, Ashley, and me, standing next to Paula Hart. It was the one where we were all smiling, not making goofy faces. You could tell that we were having a great time.

Principal Love took down the picture of Emily and handed it to my dad. I looked over at Emily. I was pretty sure that this was going to upset her. But Emily is full of surprises.

She gave me a big smile.

"Katherine and I are really proud of you," she said.

Katherine flicked her long tongue at me and hissed.

"Well, at least I am," Emily said.

Principal Love tacked up our picture right in the center of the bulletin board, where Emily's had been. Next to it, he placed a sign that said STUDENTS OF THE MONTH.

I let those words roll around

in my head. In my whole life,
I never thought I would even
be a Student of the Minute
or Student of the Hour. And
now, here I was, standing in
the hall, staring up at a picture
of me as a Student of the
Month.

All I could say was WOW.

And then I said it twelve
more times.

Wow. Wow. Wow. Wow.
Wow. Wow. Wow. Wow. Wow.
Wow. Wow. Wow.

And once more for luck.
Wow.

Each family took a picture
in front of the bulletin board.
Frankie stood with his family

and held his hands over his head like an Olympic champion. Ashley's family stood holding hands. Then it was time for the Zipzer family photograph.

"Hank, stand as close to your picture as you can," my mom said.

"And make sure you don't block it," my dad added.

"Dad, I'm not tall enough," I said, and we all laughed.

"Do you want me to take the picture?" Emily asked. I think she was remembering when I was the one who took a picture of her. I remembered how that felt, how it hurts to be left out.

"No," I said to her. "I want you to be in the picture, too."

She smiled and scooted in next to me.

"Just make sure you look like the proud little sister," I whispered.

"I'll be glad to take your family photo," Principal Love said. "I've been known to snap a prizewinner or two."

We lined up in front of the bulletin board—my mom, my dad, Emily, Katherine, Papa Pete, and me.

"Everybody say 'Student of the Month,'" Principal Love called out.

Before Principal Love snapped
the picture, Papa Pete pulled
down the zipper of his sweatshirt
just enough to show Cheerio's
entire face.

He was smiling really big.
And I was, too.

CHAPTER 12

All in all, it was a great day. There was the photo. There was the pizza party afterward with all our families. There was the mint-chip ice cream for dessert.

And let's not forget the whipped cream with the cherry on top.

By the time I got into bed, I was as tired as a bear in the middle of winter.

"Knock, knock," I heard my mom say just outside my door.

"Come in," I said, with a yawn.

She pushed the door open, came in, and sat down on the edge of my bed, tucking the covers up under my chin like she used to do when I was little.

"You should feel great right now," she said.

"I do," I answered. "Can you believe that my picture is hanging on the bulletin board in the hallway of PS 87? I never thought that would happen."

"But you see, honey, it did," she said softly. "Everything you do, Hank, you do in your own way. That's your gift."

"Yeah, but a lot of times, that gift gets me into trouble."

"You're very special," she

whispered. "Never forget that."

She gave me a kiss on the forehead and left the room.

I heard the door click behind her and felt my eyes get heavy. I felt good all over. The last thought I had before I drifted off to sleep was *Hank Zipzer, someday you're going to be somebody.*